I Had Seen Castles

Cynthia Rylant

I Had Seen

Castles

Harcourt
Brace &
Company

SAN DIEGO

NEW YORK

LONDON

The author wishes to thank Larry Peacock for his help with
historical aspects of this novel, and to extend special thanks
to Studs Terkel for writing *The Good War*.

Excerpt from "The Solitary Man" from *Selected Poems of Rainer
Maria Rilke* by Robert Bly, copyright © 1981 by Robert Bly,
reprinted by permission of HarperCollins Publishers Inc.

First paperback edition 1995

Library of Congress Cataloging-in-Publication Data
Rylant, Cynthia.
I had seen castles/Cynthia Rylant.
p.   cm.
Summary: Now an old man, John is haunted by memories of
enlisting to fight in the Second World War, a decision which
forced him to face the horrors of war and changed
his life forever.
ISBN 0-15-238003-5
ISBN 0-15-200374-6 (pbk.)
1. World War, 1939-1945—Juvenile fiction.
[1. World War, 1939-1945—Fiction.] I. Title.
PZ7.R982Iad   1993
[Fic]—dc20   92-42325

The text was set in Palatino.

Designed by Camilla Filancia
Printed in the United States of America
F E D C B A
I H G F   (pbk.)

For JTS *(1925–1967)*

and his friends

No, what my heart will be is a tower,

And I will be right out on its rim:

nothing else will be there, only pain

and what can't be said, only the world.

—RAINER MARIA RILKE
from "The Solitary Man"

I Had Seen Castles

Pittsburgh was darkness. The taste of smoke in one's throat and heavy smog and black soot. That was Pittsburgh.

I grew up there. It was the only world I knew until I was eighteen, and I never questioned the filth. Perhaps no one did, believing filth to be the price one paid for the steel and railroads that fed us our meat at dinner. Industry gave the city shiny black Fords and millionaires and lights. The lights burned at high noon as well as at midnight, so thick were the black clouds hanging above the town. They were beautiful lights, nonetheless.

The mills would ultimately poison or maim or kill most of those who worked in them. Wives would collapse in grief. Children would cry softly in their narrow little beds.

The mills were fed coal and men so Pittsburgh might live. And it did. Very well.

We lived in one of the established, older, well-trimmed neighborhoods. Our house, like all of the houses there, was big. Big and comfortable, like a soft-smelling grandmother. Carpets had not become fashionable and so the floors were left bare, glorious oak floors graced here and there by floral rugs. Floors that announced the life of the house, that resonated each tapping heel, each clickety-clack of a dog running through, every boy's oxford shoes. Floors that sang.

We had a large kitchen, all white cabinets and a long row of windows that looked out upon an enormous backyard. Imagine being a boy sitting there in that windowed room with a plate of hot pancakes. It is winter. And imagine yet again this same boy in summer and all of those windows flung open and a bowl of sweet peaches in heavy cream to eat.

One did not so much mind the dark and the dirt. One hardly minded at all.

Climb a wide wooden staircase with thick railings you can lean your whole weight against and never fear breaking, and you will be on the second floor, among the bedrooms. The father and mother's room is very near the top of the stairs, to the left. In it are a walnut turned-post bed and white curtains and a pink chenille spread and photographs of the sort found in galleries. These are much treasured by the mother. Evidence of the father's taste lies behind the glass doors of a bookcase. Theory. Darwin. Empiricism. Words to bind you to this room, this house, this planet. Words to make sense of everything.

Farther down the hall, to the left, is the nursery. Once there was a baby there, and this was not so long ago. But the baby died and the door stays softly shut.

Down the opposite hall are the rooms of those children who do live—and rather noisily. One of them is a beautiful girl, twenty years old now and still at home. She attends the university and plans to be a teacher. The room is filled with stuffed animals, and the tiny figures of ballerinas, and romance novels. She is a romantic girl. Not yet a woman. Living at home and waiting for something.

The last room, at the end of the hall, belongs to me. And here I become blank, surprised, dulled. I would tell you what it held, the year I was seventeen, if I could remember. I might guess there would have been a handsome set of encyclopedias. There must have been a globe. Surely an old air rifle or perhaps a bow with a few tattered arrows. Was there a trophy of one kind or another? A class photo? A coin collection?

This boy's room is empty, I say to anyone who might be standing just outside, in the hallway. *The boy's room is empty*, I say.

And that is when I lift myself up. Up, off the floor, and I fly through that boy's open window, cutting through the thick soot in the sky until, gasping, I am above the filth and the factories and I glide in a clear blue heaven on and on and on until I am somewhere I remember. Someplace where I can find a room and those things of mine which it holds—lovely things—and I am years away from 1942 and seventeen and the room I no longer see.

One afternoon in 1939—which season I cannot say, though I do remember the sun was shining—my father came home early from the university. I arrived from school about three o'clock, so I suppose it must have been around that time, for he nearly followed me through the door.

It was his face.

It is almost impossible for a parent to hold a secret from a child. Children, without the skills of language, spend years developing instead an intuition. By the time they are fifteen, as I was, they are masters of a kind of clairvoyance that tells them, *He is depressed*, *He is frightened*, *He is pleased*.

On any other day I could have read my father's face. But not this day, this day in 1939 when even the black smog could not block the sun's determination to shine. His was a look I had no experience of. And because of this, I followed him.

He walked into the parlor, where my mother sat with—was it embroidery?—and she smiled up at him, but his look did not change, so she laid down her sewing and waited. We waited.

"Robert?" my mother said. A question.

I leaned against the door frame, watching my father sink rather slowly into the velveteen rocker his mother had left him when she died. My father: thin, intense, honest. I had always liked him.

He looked at me, then he looked at my mother, and then he said, "We are in serious trouble."

What my mother must have thought I cannot guess, though all I could imagine was destitution. It was what everyone feared, so recently scarred by the depression, and immediately I saw myself in one of those Oklahoma jalopies, a dusty wide-brimmed hat pushed back from my forehead, several chickens in crates, heading for California. My mother, the photographer, had shown me pictures of such people. I had only to insert my own face.

And then my father explained our serious trouble.

"The Germans believe they have discovered a method of splitting the uranium atom."

It is now over fifty years later. I am becoming what I once thought of as an old man. And I want desperately to have that sunny afternoon in 1939 back. I want to have the morning. The walk to school with the guys, the banter, the wisecracking, the cuffing and shoving that boys must do to claim ownership of each other. I want to have Science and History and English and Gym, and I want to sit among my friends eating soggy sandwiches and making wild claims of one sort or another.

I want to walk home, slow and sleepy, and look forward to shutting the door of my room and lying back on my bed and hearing the thoughts in my head.

And when finally I walk through the front door of my dear old house, I want my mother to be doing her embroidery in the parlor, I want the sun to be shining, and I want my father away, away at the university, where he has not read the scientific journal that tells him something I want not to be, not ever to be, and I will make those pages disappear for him. His face will be the face I understand. And he will be home at five.

More than fifty years later, hundreds of miles between Pittsburgh and my home in Toronto, and God knows how many altered faces since . . . still I want to remake that day.

Toronto is at its best in the morning. It is the city of good manners, and breakfast is its most mannerly hour. I live in an old Victorian house on Beverley, and each morning I sit in my small courtyard off the kitchen, where I read the *Sun* and drink strong Irish coffee and spread blackberry preserves on a fresh baguette. The baguette I have purchased from a small bakery near the art gallery. The bakers there know me. I believe they like me.

The sky is clean and clear. The women are

beautiful. The men well dressed. Everyone seems healthy.

The university lies just around the corner, and there is a strength in its old stone buildings, a lovely endurance. The young students who ride their bicycles up and down College Avenue are open like flowers and they make me happy.

I was a literature professor at the university until this year. This year I retired. I am not so sure about it, for with retirement has come a reflectiveness that I do not completely welcome. If it brought reveries of wonderful students I've known, plays I've seen, writers I've read, women I've loved . . . they would be a comfort. But I cannot pull myself out of 1942. Pittsburgh. Mother and Dad. And Ginny.

They are asking that I remember them. Not as they were before or after. But as they were then. As we all were then. In the time before I went away.

When, two years after my father's revelation about the Germans, Japanese bombs dropped on Hawaii, I was dozing in my room after church and dreaming of women. Barely seventeen, I seemed able to think of nothing else but the female body, and even after an hour of Episcopal exhortations to remain holy, my subconscious betrayed my lust and I drifted in the land of long, smooth legs and perfumed skin. I was not a selective boy. In my waking hours I could as easily swoon over the cheap women working the docks as over the fresh-faced girls selling powdered doughnuts for their wheezing, suspicious fathers. Women obsessed me, and in my dreams I would find myself at the mercy of hundreds of them, all starving for a man, all rough and savage, insatiable.

"Oh, my God!" is what I heard my mother utter downstairs that Sunday afternoon. The radio knob was adjusted. I lifted my head and listened.

"Oh, my God," I whispered, and I stumbled downstairs to be with my mother.

How can I tell you what that day was for us? Stillness. We were like children suddenly slapped, and with stunned expressions we stared at our radios in profound disbelief that this was happening. That our country had been bombed.

And for the parents of young men and teenage boys, it was a nightmare. Hitler's ongoing devastation of Europe and the Japanese aggression in the Pacific had already moved President Roosevelt to enact a peacetime registration for the draft. All men ages twenty-one to thirty-six were expected to comply. The world was going crazy all around us, and had been for some time. Tons of bombs had fallen on London as we ate our Sunday dinners and washed our family dogs, and, mostly, we wanted nothing to do with it. We wanted no bombs. Parents wanted their boys home. Children needed their fathers. We all hoped to live.

That Sunday, December 7, our lives were completely altered. We were under siege of war, and we were in trouble, and nothing we did—rising, working, sleeping—would be done quite the same way again.

My parents knew this. And they had a young man in their house—me—so that Sunday the terror in their hearts must have been barely endurable. And a part of them must have wished I had been born, in some way, deformed. That I had been, growing up, perhaps slightly maimed. That I was not well nor ever could be. They must have lamented my excellent health that day. Their strong child.

And when the country's stillness was done, we all turned toward rage.

My best friend, Tony, phoned me about an hour after the broadcast.

"I'm joining up," he said. Tony, who loved the head cheerleader and vanilla malts.

"What?" I said. Tony was still a senior, as was I. Tony couldn't join up.

"Hell, yeah. I'm eighteen. To hell with those despicable little yellow insects. I'm signing up tomorrow."

"Your parents are letting you go?" I asked. It had to be just male trumpeting, I thought. Just bluster. Tony couldn't go.

"Hell, yeah. They're as pissed as I am."

And that, I suppose, is the best word to describe the emotion in every living room, kitchen, bedroom, every inhabited set of four walls in this country.

Pissed.

Every man I knew wanted to fight. My father, all my uncles, the mailman (who was already gone), the grocer (who was packing), the boys in my senior class. Everyone. The bombs that dropped on Hawaii sent a shock wave straight into the outraged soul of every man in America, and like Neanderthals, we had a primitive, fearless, screaming desire to kill.

Only weeks before, I remember, my friends and I had been at Danny's, the local hangout, vowing not to fight if the country was stupid enough to get itself dragged into a war with the Germans or the Japanese. England, France,

Russia, China . . . let them fight their own fight, we had said.

Frank Sklarek announced, "We can just go to the woods and live if Roosevelt declares war."

"Yeah," said Tony. "There are places in Pennsylvania they'd never find us. We could set up camp. Hell, it'd be just like Boy Scouts."

"No women, though," I said. "Hard to give up women."

"Better to give up women," said Jimmy Buchanan soberly, "than a couple of good legs. Plus what goes with 'em."

So we spent most of the evening plotting how to escape from our patriotic duty to fight if called upon, and not more than a month later we were all asking our parents if we could drop out of school and enlist.

Yes, I wanted to go. I wanted to go with Tony, and if Tony wasn't waiting until graduation, I didn't want to wait either. I could lie about my age. I wasn't that far from eighteen anyway. If I went with Tony, I told my parents that night at the dinner table, then we'd be all right. We'd look out for each other. We'd come home together after we'd destroyed the Japs, I said.

These words I spoke in our white, many-windowed kitchen. I remember the words. I remember the moment. My sister, Diane, sitting across the table in the dark blue dress she'd worn to church that morning and in our afternoon shock had forgotten to change out of. Slender. Dark, sparkling eyes. The sister all my friends wanted to marry. News of the bombing had brought her natural sensitivity to its height, and she fairly trembled with emotion as we talked.

Dinner was spaghetti. I remember. I remember that my mother had intended to make chicken parmigiana, but since the news she had wandered from one room to the next and forgotten the chicken. The spaghetti sauce was rather thin. There was a simple salad. A loaf of Italian bread. Glasses of iced tea. I remember the food. I just can't remember anyone eating it.

My mother said to me, "John, do you know what you are saying? You have no idea what you are saying. You're too young." Looking at my father: "He's too young."

My father, torn between an angry desire for vengeance against the Japanese and a father's duty to guide and protect his son, could not articulate why I was too young, other than to remind my mother that I was still only seventeen and could not sign up without her permission. As if that settled it.

But I was ready to go to war, and, of course, it was *war* I was too young for, war we were all too young for, and the reality of that is what we could not find at our dinner table. I can see us now, as we were, and I see the fog around us. We cannot see any horror for ourselves, for Tony, for Frank, for the mailman, or for the grocer. We deceive ourselves into believing we can clean up the enemy, put him back in his place, and have our chicken parmigiana another night. Soon. A quick war and, intact, we all sit down again to eat.

I met Ginny falling off a bus. And that may be the simplest thing I will ever be able to say about her.

Once Pittsburgh and the rest of the country had lived through the first agonizing twenty-four hours after the attack on Hawaii—terrified the rest of us might be blown apart at any minute as well—the next step was to organize as a nation at war. Today one sees the same sort of response after natural disasters. The small plains town pulling itself together once the tornado has roared through. Earthquake survivors holding each other in wounded corners of California neighborhoods. Everyone is out of the house, and the barriers that once kept them apart—walls, fences, grudges—have disappeared.

Multiply that unity a thousand times, and you have America after a surprise bombing by a tiny Oriental nation noted in the U.S., until the attack, only for its laughably cheap imports. "Made in Japan" in those days meant that whatever you had in your hand would fall to pieces in a matter of hours. Being bombed by a country we regarded as so thoroughly inferior to our own brought on the angry roar of a bull who has just been bitten by a housefly.

For a while we lived under threat of surprise attack, appointed air-raid wardens in our towns, and if sirens went off, hung blackout paper in our windows so the bombs might not find us. Pittsburgh's lovely lights went out— *click*. Schoolchildren (including me) memorized the silhouettes of Japanese fighter planes (we had purchased paperbacks with their illustrations), and we kept our wary young eyes toward the sky. Anyone Oriental was regarded with great suspicion, and in fact, every stranger, no matter the race, was considered possibly threatening. "Shhhhh!" warned the war posters. "Spies are lurking."

Everything became desperate; all decisions profound, all emotions fierce.

Love in those times was nuts. Not artificial, not ridiculous. No, it was so real as to be completely heartbreaking. But it was nuts all the same.

And I fell off a crazy bus in that crazy world and landed at the feet of this remarkable girl.

I fell from the bus because someone had pushed me. On every bus in Pittsburgh in 1942 was a kind of miniature mob. Gasoline was being rationed, and tires, and patriotically we were all trying to take the bus. But we, meaning the locals, were not the only flag-waving citizens trying to take a bus from one end of town to the other. Pittsburgh was being overrun by an influx of employment seekers. Swarms of outsiders were flowing into the city to take advantage of the war industry, which had turned up the heat of the steel mills to full blast, escalated the volume of the factories to a high-pitched scream. There was work and work and work to be had. People came, hungry for it. Ginny's father came.

And I fell off the bus. It was July 1942.

"Are you all right?"

I looked up into the most hypnotic blue eyes I had ever seen. Ginny was what they call Dark Irish. Thick black hair, pale freckled skin, and blue eyes to pin you to the ground. She smiled and offered me her hand.

In today's time it may be difficult to understand the significance of a young woman offering her hand to a young man lying on the ground in complete prostration. Women frequently hold doors open for men these days. They have held them open for me. I am still a bit shy about it, though I accept as graciously as I am able. But in '42, women did not hold doors and they did not pull sheepish young men to their feet.

Stunned by the blueness of her eyes, I took the hand Ginny offered, and sure enough, she hauled me up. Thank god the bus was already well down the street and no one had seen.

Rubbing the elbow I'd fallen on and trying to appear nonchalant about my public humiliation, I replied casually, "The guy with the suitcase pushed me."

"I saw him," Ginny said, looking much more put out about it than I. "The stupid jackass."

I wonder now how many feet my jaw

dropped. Young women, Dark Irish or not, simply did not refer to men with suitcases in time of war as jackasses. At least, not the women in my strongly Episcopalian-Presbyterian–Watch-your-mouth-young-man neighborhood. How could I not love Ginny after this?

I grinned. She grinned.

"Were you trying to get on?" I asked, pushing my fingers through my hair and working into a sophisticated slouch.

"No. Just got off," she answered.

"You were on the bus, too?"

"Yeah. Behind the hillbilly with the guitar."

I'd seen no hillbilly with a guitar. But as I said, the buses at that time were positively packed, three to a seat, the aisles full. The man who pushed me had been sitting on his suitcase in the middle of the aisle. He was probably trying to scramble into an empty seat while we were unloading and in his haste knocked me right out the door.

I had everything figured out now. Everything except how to get to know this girl. Then I remembered the magic question with which one opened every new conversation in 1942:

"Do you have someone in the war?"

By this time we were both walking west and she seemed to be assuming I was going her way. I wasn't—or at least, I wasn't until that moment. I should have been walking east, to the university, where I was filling in part-time in my father's physics department. Every place needed extra labor, with the men away. I was working for free, grading exams. It seemed the right thing to do at the time.

Ginny shook her head and smiled ruefully.

"No," she answered. "No one in the war. Unless you count sixteen-hour days and two-thousand-degree temperatures and idiots with ladles of molten iron trying not to bump into each other. Unless you count that."

She gave me a frustrated look and tossed back her hair. Lovely hair, lying on her shoulders.

"You have someone in the mills? Your dad?" I asked.

She nodded.

"We moved here last month," she began to explain as I took her elbow and guided her across Fifth Avenue. I did this instinctively, believing she had forgotten her surroundings. As she spoke, she was with her father, in the mill.

"From where?" I asked.

"Smithville," she said.

"Where?"

"Smithville." She grinned. "You know,

near Craley. Down the road from Bart."

"Oh, right," I answered. "Smithville. The one beside . . . um . . . Burt."

"Bart," she corrected.

"It's a great town," I said. "You must be so proud."

"Enormously," she answered.

Grinning our ears off, we crossed another street.

I still remember that word she used: *enormously*. I don't know that I'd ever heard a girl use it in that way. And it seemed, well, *male*. Cocky and strong. I wished I'd said it instead. If I had said it, I would have used it this way: *I like you—enormously*.

We walked on and I learned that Ginny, her parents, and her two small brothers had all moved to Pittsburgh when the factories shifted into high gear. It is difficult to comprehend today, in this highly militarized time, but when the U.S. declared war against Japan and, soon after, against Germany, our army was thirty-ninth in the world in terms of power. It was still using horses to pull its artillery. Boys' slender rifles. Little jeeps with jaunty little guns.

After the Nazis decimated our pitiful army a few times with their monstrous panzer tanks and eighty-millimeter machine guns, it occurred to us that we were—as we had known from the start, but not until now so cruelly—in very serious trouble. We needed weapons. Devastating weapons. And a lot of them, fast.

I met Ginny in July. Apart from my father, who at fifty was considered too old to enlist, I was, at that time, losing all the men in my life to war. One by one they packed up and left. Tony had already gone, without me. Other friends were, like me, simply marking time until their eighteenth birthdays. My life slipped and shifted each time someone I knew climbed aboard a crowded Greyhound and headed for boot camp. I was lonely. And I knew there was a chance I might die in this war. I wasn't at all sure of any future, so I wanted a life as quickly as possible, before it was my turn to board the last bus out. I wanted a *life*.

"So, would you like to go to the movies sometime?" I asked Ginny as we walked. Brazenly. Fearlessly. I had a hell of a lot more to fear than a pretty girl's rejection. I didn't feel the luxury of time and subtle courtship; I had to start things *now*.

"Sure," she said.

And that is how we began.

When I was nine years old, my father brought home for me one day a wooden castle set. All of the pieces were left unfinished, so it was my job to decorate everything with thick paint and then put it together. All of the castle essentials were there: battlements, palisades, baileys. Even some small, sturdy knights awaiting their colors.

I closed myself up in my room and did not come out for hours. In that time I fell deeply in love with castles and their secrets. And I wanted to see the real thing, to go to Europe and walk through a castle cut from heavy stone and let myself believe it was mine.

I played with my wooden castle and knights for many years, then when childhood was done, my mother carefully packed each bailey, each battlement, each sturdy knight into a cardboard box and stored everything in the basement. She marked the box, simply, CASTLE.

I moved that box countless times in my life until the day I left home. Searching for Christmas lights, I saw it: CASTLE. Rummaging through sports equipment for an old softball: CASTLE. Carrying down boxes of summer clothes, carrying up boxes of winter ones, each trip to the basement: CASTLE.

Did I somehow know then that the word would have real meaning for me one day? That when I looked at the word on the box, I was looking at my future?

When I met Ginny, the steady routine of my comforting family life had already begun to disappear. In late June my father took a leave of absence from the university because he had been called to work in California at UCLA. He explained to us that he was needed to develop defense technology and admitted that he had no idea exactly what he would be working on. But he had been asked to go, so he set forth to do his job and left my mother and my sister and me to our own tasks.

My mother signed on at a local factory that ordinarily manufactured automobile parts but had been converted to make artillery pieces and small arms. The first day I saw her in slacks, her hair tied up in a bandanna, I was—and this is very hard to admit—repulsed. I had seen her in a dress every day of my life and I liked her femininity, her difference from my father. I loathed those slacks she wore, and when she came home drawn and exhausted after a ten-hour day of numbing assembly-line work, I felt orphaned. Truly. I respected her patriotic motives, but I wanted a *mother*.

What I did not understand then, and didn't understand for literally decades afterward, was that my mother was motivated precisely by *being* my mother. The government held that the only way to win the war, and thus quickly *end* the war, was to out-manufacture the enemy. To produce ten times the tanks and artillery the enemy possessed. Do this—produce—and the war will be over.

My mother wanted her only son to be spared

this war. She wanted to save his life. For ten miserable, backbreaking hours a day, six days a week, my mother worked as if she could singlehandedly wipe the Germans and the Japanese off the face of the earth, and by doing so, keep this boy alive.

And I resented her slacks.

So, by the summer of '42, my father was on the West Coast, my mother was at work, I was distractedly waiting for a birthday, and my sister, Diane, was in hot water up to her neck.

Pittsburgh, in those first months of war, was an immensely grim place. The entire country was grim. We were not ready for war, and every day there were military setbacks. We were losing, and it gave us a devastated, helpless feeling.

Like all American cities, Pittsburgh was swarming with young men who wandered like lost puppies, waiting. Waiting in peace to be sent to a violent hell. These boys needed women. The soft comfort of them, the intimate talk. Sex, too, but this was not nearly as important as a woman's mere *presence*.

My sister, Diane, was soft and kind and beautiful and single, and suddenly she became the most important girl in the world to about five different boys, all of whom were readying to go to war.

How could she say no when they asked her to a movie, to a dance, to walk along the city streets with them? She could not say no. She was kind, and she would offer them her hand and would talk and dance and stroll because she could not see choosing anything else.

"Someone called for you last night," my mother would tell Diane at breakfast.

"Who?" Diane would ask.

"Let's see," my mother would say, "I'm trying to remember the boy's name."

"Bill?"

"No."

"Jimmy?"

"No."

"Cecil?"

"No."

And Diane would continue her roll call until a name fit.

But matters soon grew increasingly complicated for her, and after only a few dates with each boy, Diane would come home distracted, worried. Her face sometimes ghost white, sometimes flushed.

She would not tell me, her seventeen-year-old brother, what was happening. But I could guess. The boys were consuming her. I knew because I was beginning to feel my own urgency. They wanted her love, her sympathy, her promises, her body. Like doomed men they wanted one last good meal so they might meet their fate strong and clear eyed. Nourished. And so they might have someone to come home to.

I could sometimes hear her weeping softly in her room. I did not know what to do for her, and I had not yet learned the simple tact of saying to someone in distress, "Is there anything I can do for you?" Perhaps she would have said yes, and perhaps I would have gone into her room and nudged aside a teddy bear or two to make a space for myself, and listened.

If I had done this, here is what I believe she would have told me:

John, they're all afraid and sometimes I see death in their faces and I think how foolish not to give them what love I have. Such a small and simple gift. I'm not sure, anymore, what morality is.

Already we had lost good neighborhood boys. We would see the gold star in the window of someone's home and walk past solemnly, our eyes averted, respectful. Morbidly I would wonder how the soldier had died: Was his death quick or long in coming, was his body brought home in one piece or many or even at all? And like the naïve and optimistic kid I was—we all were—I had to believe, of course, that I would be luckier than that.

I took for granted that I would go to war, though I was still below the draft age, which then was twenty-one. In the summer of '42 I was not yet trapped, at least not legally, and I suppose I could have consoled myself with the thought that the war would probably be over by the time I was old enough to be called.

But in that zealous time there was no question that you were not considered a man unless you signed up. No question that you would be regarded with utter contempt and loathing if you chose not to volunteer. In the window of the barbershop a few blocks from our house was a crudely lettered sign that read, No Yellow Bellies, Skunks, or COs Allowed, and that sums up pretty well the sentiment of most people toward any able-bodied young men who had no stomach for killing. Men who called themselves conscientious objectors.

I was nearly eighteen. I *needed* to affirm my manhood, my worth. I could not risk the debilitating shame of being labeled a coward.

And it was my definition of cowardice, and Ginny's, that would so penetrate every part of our relationship until, at the end, we would finally see ourselves with painful clarity. And each would wish the other were someone else.

Ginny's family lived in a storeroom above a small food market, and when first I saw their home I could feel the rush of hot blood to my face. I was embarrassed for them.

Ginny had not wanted me to pick her up for our date. On the phone she urged me to just meet her at the movie theater. But a stubbornness came over me for some reason, an unfamiliar bullheadedness, and I insisted that I pick her up and meet her parents. Perhaps it was just the intensity of the times. Very little seemed casual.

I found the market with no trouble. I simply took a bus toward a tattered neighborhood beside the river and got off. I had lived in Pittsburgh all my life and never walked these particular streets. I'd never made a friend who wasn't from my side of town. And in the midst of squalor, I felt uncomfortable at being so tidy, so clean. I wanted a bus to roar by and cover me with mud.

I found the market, I found the door, I knocked, and Ginny let me in.

I walked into a towel.

The room had been strung with clotheslines, and shirts, towels, underwear, pillowcases hung like flags all around me. First lesson: how the poor do laundry.

And this will tell you about Ginny. She did not apologize. She stood straight and looked directly at me, and she said, "John, this is my mother, Louise Burton."

Louise Burton, thin, pale, weary, smiled and shook my hand. I dreaded she might make reference to their poverty in such terms as, *I'm sorry we've nothing better to offer*, or, *Please forgive the laundry*, or, *Excuse our dreary home*, but she spared me that and said simply, "How nice to meet you, John." And I believe she meant it.

Ginny's father was at the mill, her two small brothers playing with some children on the corner; thus I was reprieved of a thorough inspection by the whole family. I told Mrs. Burton how glad I was to meet her, where I was taking her daughter, and when we would be back; and then we left. The market downstairs gave the whole building the smell of bananas, though I doubt there were actually any there. Fresh fruit was increasingly hard to come by. Perhaps the smell had permeated the wood of the place over the years. Perhaps it would smell of bananas forever. I hope that it has.

Ginny looked beautiful. She was wearing a simple yellow dress—how clearly I see it now—and flat black shoes. No nylons. We were making gunpowder instead of nylons. Her hair shone black. Her lips were painted red. I looked at her and felt short of breath.

We caught the bus downtown, and I expect we rode in a stupor. Both of us out of our element. But when we finally emerged from that hot, tight bus into the life of the city, we breathed easily and laughed and began taking those small steps by which we might find each other.

I'd planned to take her to a movie, but we

never made it. We stopped at a coffee shop, made the mistake of opening our mouths. We didn't shut up for four hours.

I don't think I had ever talked so much in my life.

Ginny continued to surprise and impress me each minute we were together. She had a voracious appetite, and she shocked me, when I offered to buy her a hamburger, by ordering two, with *double onions!* When she saw the apparent look of dismay on my face, she said, "If you order the same thing we'll smell alike and it won't matter." So I did. And it didn't.

We hadn't sat for five minutes before the talk turned to war, as it would.

"I suppose you're going to enlist," Ginny said matter-of-factly, popping a pickle into her mouth. There was something in her voice I didn't understand, and I hesitated before answering.

"Sure," I said. "Of course. In August."

And here is what I expected: I expected her eyes to go soft, her hand to reach across to mine. I expected her to say bravely, *I know you must. I wish it were not so. But I know you must.* And I would be her hero.

But she pursed her lips and nodded her head and rather nonchalantly looked out the window.

Wait. Something's wrong, I thought. Have I made her *angry?* I felt that I had, but I didn't know how to find out. So I left it there—enlisting—and we didn't talk of it the rest of the evening.

We talked of a million other things instead:

"Are you religious?" she asked. She had just ordered a second strawberry shake.

"Well, uh, yes. I think so. But I'm not sure exactly what you mean by *religious*."

"Do you go to church?" she asked.

"Yes."

"Because you have to or because you want to? If your parents didn't expect you to go, would you anyway?"

"Well . . ." I had never considered this. I took a moment to imagine waking on a Sunday, knowing it was Sunday, and choosing sleep.

"Yes," I realized as I said it. "Yes, I'd go anyway."

"Really?" She was surprised.

I shrugged.

"It feels normal to me. It feels right to go."

She smiled.

"What about you?" I asked. "Would you go alone, on your own?"

"No," she said.

"You aren't religious?"

"I'm very religious."

"But you wouldn't go."

"Won't go," she answered. "Don't go."

"Why?" I asked.

"I just don't like God in a suit."

We talked:

"What was your life like in Smithville?" I asked.

"I could breathe," she answered. I knew that she meant this in many ways.

"We lived in my grandmother's big house. My father hadn't found any work for a long time. Then the war, the mills begging for people. So we had to follow him. My mother felt we should follow him. I vomited all the way to Pittsburgh." She grinned wryly.

"What's your father like?" she said.

This surprised me. No one had ever asked me this question. Everyone knew what my father was like.

"He's in love with science," I answered.

"That's good," she said.

"What?"

"He loves what he's made of."

"And your father?" I asked. "What's he like?"

A sad look on her face.

"I never see him. I have trouble remembering. He leaves at dawn and works till midnight." She sighed. "He wants to make enough money to buy us a house. He says the war might give us a house."

When she said this, I felt deeply uncomfortable. I didn't know why, what it meant, so I buried it. A mistake. It would be back. Her short explanation of her father's turning the war to his advantage would settle deep inside me, and much later, later when I was no longer the boy I was, it would mix with larger things and rise up again.

"He looks very bad," she said quietly.

Living among steel mills, I knew the look she spoke of, though until that moment I don't believe I ever cared about the person who bore it or the circumstances that created it. I did not understand exploitation, did not value the sacredness of human life. Looking back, it is as if Ginny were laying out lessons one by one for me to learn, to report back to her later. As if sitting there she signified all the important ways in which I had not grown up.

But none of this mattered that evening. In

lovely ignorance of my shortcomings, I sat in her presence and glowed with satisfaction. We were hitting it off.

We talked until ten, then rode the bus back to her place above the market. Her street was gray and possessed of a kind of sadness. I didn't want to leave her there. I wanted to take her home with me, to my beautiful home, and put her between clean sheets, smooth back her hair, talk her softly to sleep. I wanted to make up for Pittsburgh.

But I made no such offer, of course, and found myself shy and excited as she turned to me to say good night, and then we were kissing, and I wanted to stay with her always.

Tony died.

I will not be very good at this. As I write I find myself looking out the window toward the street, and I think surely I should walk to the market for oranges, see the new exhibit at the gallery, catch the Altman film at the cinema. There is something that needs doing besides this. Besides writing that Tony died.

No one close to me had ever died before. I try to remember the boy I was then, the one unfamiliar with death, and it is very difficult. I have to let fall years of living, put away most

41

of my life, to find him again. I have to look at the trees and the houses and remember what it is to know only this, to know only a neighborhood of kind people and tidy homes and the freedom of bicycles.

Tony died, and it was months before his remains were shipped home to his family, and by that time I was gone. So I cannot describe that homecoming or his being laid to rest.

Here is what I do remember: looking for him. Not in the familiar places. Not on his front porch or at Danny's or on the street in his Chevy. Tony had been away long enough that in these places I no longer expected to find him.

I found myself looking instead toward the hills. My eyes would search the tops of the hills surrounding Pittsburgh, and I would realize that he wasn't up there. Sometimes my eyes looked as far to the horizon as possible and I said to myself, "He isn't there." I'd look at groves of trees and long highways and the three rivers leading out to the world and know he wasn't there anywhere, and then, then I would believe he was dead. But sometimes I just could not accept this, and I felt that if I just *thought* about him hard enough, I would bring him back. I would think him back and set him on the firm ground and undo what had been done.

My family grieved for Tony with an intense sorrow I had not imagined they would feel. My mother's face was tearstained for days. My father's voice cracked when he called on the phone, and some nights he couldn't finish a conversation. Diane, who loved Tony best of all of my friends, wept during the day and then in the evening masked the traces of loss with powder and mascara and lipstick and smiled for the new enlistee at the door. A determined smile.

The few friends from my senior class who were still biding their time until they were of age were quiet. Stoic. Speculating that Tony had just been in the wrong place at the wrong time, maybe made a wrong move and wound up dead. They would be sure to make the right moves. They'd watch their backs and stand in the right places. They'd be more careful than he.

And I think we all finally, deeply, understood that we really were at war. And that our side might not win. If Tony could die, then we really might not win.

Tony's death terrified me. He was the strongest boy I'd known, and if he could not survive combat, it was difficult to have any faith that I might. This was overwhelming, too strong to quell, so instead I rolled it up into a tight little ball and transformed it into something else. I transformed it into an aching need for Ginny.

Her parents had no phone, so I found myself constantly taking crowded buses and walking slimy streets as if I'd been born to it. I grew used to this. I grew used to so many different things that indeed I stopped living my real life altogether. It would be a long, long time before I would find what I might call a real life again.

Though I saw Ginny's father only once—on a Sunday afternoon when I happened upon him and his boys throwing a ball in the street—I believed he was a good man. I thought him good that particular day because, exhausted as he must have been and wanting only to sleep all of a Sunday, he played instead with his children. I thought him good because he wanted a house for his family and was willing to labor like an animal to secure one. And I thought him good because he was not miserly and gave a bit of his money to Ginny so she might buy herself a new blouse or hair ribbons and so look pretty for me, whom he knew she wanted very much to please.

And though all of the heroes of that time wore military uniforms, then (and even more so now) I regarded Ginny's father as heroic. And I liked her all the more because of him.

Ginny did not have a lot to say when I told her of Tony's death. She was strangely quiet, though sympathetic, and in my mind I made of her quietness a profound respect for a fallen soldier. I imagined her reverent, as I was. She was silent, I told myself, because the nobility of his sacrifice was beyond language.

And then one day as we walked along Forbes Avenue, browsing in bookstores, she asked me if I had given any thought to registering, in the event I was drafted, as a CO.

"What?" I said, stunned. We stood in front of a shop that had a poster in its window: Choke the Japs.

Ginny raised her eyebrows.

"It's just a question," she said with a tone of annoyance. "I mean, you're still not in danger of being drafted, so it's not as if you have to seriously take a stand right now. I just wondered, that's all."

"Ginny, I could *never* be a conscientious objector! *Never!*"

I don't know whether I waved my arms dramatically in the air, but as I remember those words, my guess is that I did.

Ginny turned her blue eyes on me.

"But why?" she asked sincerely.

Why.

I could not articulate then, in any way that she would have understood, why I would rather have *died* than been judged a coward. There are no words for such emotion as I felt, such overwhelming singlemindedness. My god, I was seventeen. I had barely learned to shave and I still trembled in bed during violent thunderstorms. So much of me was yet unfinished, including the ability to explain my feelings. I *felt*, and I followed a feeling to its end. It was the best I could do.

"For freedom," I told her. "To keep our country free. To *protect* us, Ginny!" I said this hotly, and as I spoke, I realized we had never confronted each other so strongly. I hated conflict. I wanted to go home and sleep instead.

"There are other ways, you know, to solve differences. We could have kept out of it," she answered.

I stared at her in disbelief. *"You're against the war?"*

She lifted her chin and firmed her mouth. "I'm against war," she said quietly. "War."

"And you think I should just wait this thing out in some CO camp in the middle of some goddamned wilderness?" I asked. "Just hide my yellow butt however many years it takes and then come back and face people?" And as I said this, I knew I could never do it. Never.

"It's not about being afraid," she said. "It's about religious choice."

"*Religious choice?*" My voice by now was loud, shrill. "Religious choice? This from someone who doesn't even go to church! What does *war* have to do with religion?"

And as I asked this absurd question, even now I remember that I knew, I *knew* what it had to do with religion. I knew the answer, but in 1942 there was no finding it.

"Nothing," Ginny said. "That's the point."

I was mute, simply rendered speechless. We were silent for a very long time, our eyes glued to the window of the shop.

Finally, Ginny said softly, "If you die, you miss everything. You won't be back and you'll miss everything."

Just as softly, I answered, "If 'everything' here is that important, then I'd damned well *better* go."

And in silence I took her home.

A week later we made love, I suppose inevitably. Sex can do wonderful things for fear.

What I had fantasized night after night as I lay awake in my bed *happened*. I took Ginny to my beautiful home, slipped her between my cool, clean sheets, smoothed back her silky dark hair, and made love to her.

I am certain that had this happened at any other time in my young life I would have fumbled, ruined the experience with nervousness and lack of grace.

But with each day, things were becoming

more and more uncertain. The daily papers were filled with frustrating stories of military catastrophe. *Life* magazine delivered bloody scenes of carnage to our door every week. There was a nearly palpable sense of mortality in the air, and always being an intuitive boy, I was completely vulnerable to it. I was not particularly good at swagger and boast. I could not say, *Hell, yeah, we'll beat 'em and I'm coming home a hero.* I was beginning to have a keen awareness of my chances, as a young man, of surviving a global war, and only this did I fear: only death.

I wasn't afraid to bring Ginny home when my mother and sister were out, wasn't afraid to undress her, wasn't afraid to touch her, and wasn't afraid of the consequences of all this. I didn't know if I'd ever be with another girl and I wasn't afraid to be with this one.

What I remember most from the experience was my absolute fascination with her beautiful breasts, and, later, being rather surprised that during intercourse we did not *psychically* merge. Somehow I had come to expect that when two people made love they shot up to a higher level of consciousness and became one. They lost themselves inside each other.

But at one point during our lovemaking, I found myself actually craving one of those great

49

spaghetti dinners at Luigi's Restaurant. And when it was done, and we lay holding each other, I caught myself singing "Battle Hymn of the Republic" in my head.

I don't mean to say that the lovemaking did not have enormous meaning for me. It did. I was simply surprised by how ordinary it could be, and how real everything remained.

Ginny lay in my arms, her head resting on my chest, and we did not speak. I guess we should have said *I love you*, and I'm certain I considered saying it. But it seemed so small a response to what was between us. It seemed Ginny deserved more than those words.

We were also trying very hard to bury our differences regarding war and peace. Talk may simply have been too dangerous. I did love her—I wanted to keep loving her—so I said nothing.

I took Ginny home, as usual on a crowded bus. She held tightly to my hand and when finally we reached her door, she turned to me, her face serious.

"Now you've gone and made this big mark," she said.

"What?" I asked.

"Before," she said, "you would have been just one of the boys I dated when I was young.

Someone whose last name I wouldn't be able to remember fifty years from now. But now you're *the* boy, you know?" She looked up at me as if we were buddies just figuring a thing out.

"And when I'm seventy, when I'm eighty," she continued, with a sad kind of smile, "I'll still remember you. I'll still remember your last name. You'll be one of the big marks in my life, like on those timelines in history . . . Columbus Discovers America, Pilgrims Land at Plymouth Rock, Civil War Ends, Ginny Burton Makes Love with John Dante."

I wanted to make some funny remark. Keep the joke going. Help her fill the terrible emptiness that comes after something for which there are no words.

But I couldn't. Her talk of the future had shaken me.

"You know, I'm still going to be here when you're eighty," I said, trying to believe it. "Maybe"—and this was quite sincere—"maybe you'll remember my last name because it will be yours, too."

Saying this was a pleasure I had not expected, for it brought forth images of a long and peaceful life for myself, images of a comfortable old house and Ginny and my parents and Diane and all of us, serene, sublime, having lived so many, many easy years.

Ginny was kind. She did not use my words as an opportunity to lead me further into commitment. Nor did she belittle my romantic response with sarcasm.

She put her soft hand against my face and she said, "You will be an old man one day, John. I'm sure of it. You will be an old man."

Here my hand begins to tremble. I am in Toronto and I am sixty-seven and my heart is breaking as I remember those words she spoke to me that day: *You will be an old man*. Ginny had no idea of the gift she gave with those words. I would remember them as if God himself had spoken. I would regard them as sacred prophecy, and later, later, when my own weak heart could not gather enough will to live, when I felt at times I would surely die and even wished to die, I would remember that Ginny had said I would one day be an old man. And I lived for her.

August 1942.

My sister, Diane, had become engaged to three enlisted men, all of them now overseas. Two of the engagements were formal—meaning that she had accepted a ring from each boy. The third engagement was less formal, no ring, yet far more binding: she was pregnant with the young man's child.

We all made such enormous leaps of faith in that time. I believe it had everything to do with our unreliable futures. We could not plot out this many years for college, then work, then marriage, then children, and so forth. We lived with a powerful sense of the *present*, and we could not postpone anything.

One boy was shipped to England, one to North Africa, one to the Pacific; and Diane had said yes to them all. I suppose it must seem terribly cruel in retrospect, but she could not disappoint. She could not. Diane accepted their rings, made promises to them all, made love to one, and waited for the future to tell her what to do next.

What the future told her one day was that she was pregnant. And what my mother told her after hearing this news was that, for her own sake, she had to leave.

We are all victims of our time and place. Even today this is true for most people, and it was fiercely true then. Our time and place had sent my father to California, from where he called us with a tired gray voice each Sunday night. So far away. Truly *distant*. It sent my mother into a factory that every few days tore the flesh off someone's arm or lacerated a finger or fractured a skull because its experienced workers were somewhere in North Africa or the Pacific and instead housewives, secretaries, old men, and farm laborers were struggling to make it work. And it sent warm Diane into the arms of a needy soldier, then off to rural Ohio, where an elderly great-aunt might shelter her from the vicious judgment she would surely have faced if she stayed home.

I still cannot believe that Diane and I never found each other in that time. That I let her pack, then went with her and my mother to the train station, and stood there waiting, sensing her fear and her loneliness. And though I loved her profoundly I could not say so, nor say anything approaching any expression of love. Her hand clung tightly to my mother's and in the eyes of each there was both anguish and resolve, and when finally my mother had to give her up, when Diane climbed on board to go off somewhere and wait for her baby alone (save the company of the unfamiliar aunt), I could only half smile and awkwardly murmur goodbye and stiffly embrace and be done.

We had slept in matching flannel pajamas as children and had loved the same mother, the same father, the same dear house, had stared at the same tall tree in our backyard on dark nights when we could not sleep, and now she was sacrificing everything she knew to the times, and I was set to lose, possibly, my life to them—and we could not talk. Could not. I was never able to tell her, later, how sorry I was for this.

She did not meet Ginny. I just didn't find the time for introductions. And perhaps it was my own discomfort with Ginny's deepening feelings against the war that dampened my enthusiasm for bringing her home to the family.

Diane left home August 3. I turned eighteen August 7. And on August 8, 1942, I enlisted in the United States Army. When I enlisted, I had never owned a car, had never rented an apartment, had never taken a trip by myself, had never smoked a cigarette, had never been drunk. The only adult experience I had known was making love with Ginny. This I had done twice. Having reached this milestone, I felt I had a definite edge over the other eighteen-year-old enlistees. Optimistically, I thought I might stand out for my exceptional maturity.

When I joined the army, my mother could not speak to me all that day without her voice breaking. She did not go to work. She felt that in her distraction she might be a risk to the others' safety. She stayed home and repaired brown patches of lawn while tears dropped off her face. She had wanted me to wait. But we both knew the draft age was bound to be lowered to eighteen soon (and it was, two months later). This way, I felt I had some choice. And it was for me a hell of a lot easier than waiting. Waiting was a nightmare for everyone. I enlisted, and there was a strength in knowing something of my future.

But Ginny felt no such comfort. She had very nearly begged on her knees that I not sign up. Until the day I enlisted, her feelings toward me had fluctuated between deep sorrow and bitter resentment. She hated me for wanting to go, for believing in the war. But she loved me too much to punish me for our differences.

When I joined the army, Ginny's desperation and anger and horror and revulsion could not be contained, and on the sidewalk in front of her family's apartment, she just exploded.

Sobbing, she said over and over, "How could you do it? How could you do it?"

I was a mess of emotion. Thrilled at the prospect of wearing a uniform and scared out of my mind I might die in it. Worried about my sister and my mother. Missing, terribly, my father. Guilt-ridden by the anguish I could see in Ginny's face. I longed for a normal life. A quiet, normal life.

"You're going to shoot *people?*" Ginny cried. "*Boys?* Just shoot them because they're from another country?"

"They're shooting us, Ginny! They killed Tony, they're killing thousands of Tonys! We didn't start this damned thing, but we've got to finish it. Finish Hitler, then finish the Japs. We have got to *win*."

Ginny looked at me. "You sound like a poster for the Marines. You sound like all that disgusting propaganda on the radio."

"It isn't propaganda," I said.

"It's all propaganda, John!" She grabbed my arm. *"Think for yourself,"* she begged. "You don't know what's behind it all. You'll be fighting for the politicians and the factory owners and everybody else who'll get something out of this. And not one of them is going to pick up a gun. John, please, please. Get out of it."

"I can't get out, Ginny. I'm in. I'm not spending the next decade in prison. I'm *in*."

Then she pushed me. Hard. If she'd been a man, I suppose she would have hit me. Instead, she pushed me away and, crying, went back inside.

Solemn, numb, I took the bus home.

When I walked into my house, the only sound was of the sparrows singing outside the kitchen window. I poured myself a glass of milk and went out to the back steps. The birds were hopping among my mother's neatly sown victory garden—which, I realized, would not be feeding me, nor my sister, nor my father. Our family had disappeared. It was the same house, same furniture, same lilacs and rosebushes. But the family had gone away.

I watched the sparrows, tears in my eyes, scared, and I asked God for help. And in that pocket of silence, there in the sun by the garden, I decided that if I did not die in the war, I would come back and find for myself a place just like this. And for the rest of my life I would sit in the sun and watch sparrows.

I saw Ginny once more before I left. I had ten days before boarding a bus for Fort Benning, Georgia, and in all this empty time, I saw her only once more.

She refused to speak to me. I left messages at the little market beneath her apartment, but Ginny would not return my calls. I took the bus to her place six days in a row, knocked, and was turned away by her mother, whose face resembled that of my own mother by this time—troubled, grieving—and politely I rode the bus back home. In the evenings my mother and I ate simple dinners and reminisced about the past. We tried not to speak too much of the war. We certainly did not speak of the future.

My mother was—at least, had been—a photographer, and she was really quite talented. I have many of her prints hanging on my walls today. I did not realize, at the time, that she had given up what must have been the most *individual* part of herself during those war years. Perhaps some of the most significant things we all lost in wartime were our passions, our eccentric interests. As the fighting continued, we became more and more generalized, like figures in stock magazine ads. My mother was no longer the photographer, the woman whose deepest wish was to meet W. Eugene Smith, the woman who loved red Chinese poppies and grew them in huge clusters in her front yard, whose favorite music was Baroque harpsichord, who braided her hair each night and looked like a little girl afterward. She was, instead, Rosie the Riveter. Reduced to a beaming advertisement for the production of artillery. My sister was no longer the young woman with ambitions of teaching in a rural one-room schoolhouse and becoming a writer someday, who loved vanilla ice cream and dogs and the poetry of Emily Dickinson. She was, instead, a soldier's girl. My absent father relished old books and sailing and could cook a delicious lasagna. He loved mystery and the earth and the stars. The war reduced him to an anonymous scientist employed by the government.

And when I enlisted, I became one of twelve million soldiers. Whoever I had been, or could now be, made no difference in the world. And I mean that quite literally: the world.

When I told my father, during his Sunday evening call, that I had enlisted, I think he stopped breathing. When finally he could inhale once again, it seemed to be with great labor. A man with a ton of weight on his heart.

He supported the war. He supported the draft—but it is one thing to believe in an idea. Quite another to give up your child to it.

He just could not say anything, anything at all. In the heavy silence I finally said, "It'll be all right, Dad. Everything will be all right."

This in '42, when everything was not all right. The Axis nations were winning by sheer brute force and the Japanese, since our naval devastation at Pearl Harbor, still dominated the Pacific. Things were very wrong yet, and my father knew this.

He said, "I wish I could go in your place, son. Please be careful. Please . . . be careful."

I said that I would. As if I would be able to judge where each mortar shell would fall and, carefully, step aside. As if I had some control over my fate. At that time, I still believed that I did have control. That I could keep myself alive. All I had to do, for me and for Dad, was to be careful.

During his calls my father never spoke of the work he was doing for the war. I assumed he was involved in developing better weapons. But he never said specifically what he was doing, nor why.

I missed him more during those ten days I was waiting to ship out than I ever had before or ever would again. His presence in a room had always had the effect of making me feel very safe, and I wanted to have him sit by me and radiate that quiet certainty and ease. Whatever he might have said to me then, I would have believed.

Upset about my enlistment as my parents were, still, their age had given them certain means of coping. They had lived through many hard times and had seen most things come out all right. They had learned to trust the workings of destiny, and they had some experience of faith. I suppose that is what wisdom is all about.

Ginny had no such resource, at so young an age, and I understand now that when I enlisted all she could respond with was raw pain. Ginny was so exceptional, so individual and real, and extremely courageous in so cowardly a time. Cowardly in the sense that dissension of any kind, any questioning of the rightness of our declaring war, was simply not tolerated. Anyone against the war was, by association, against the young soldiers fighting it, and therefore without conscience. Protesters were beaten and abused. There could be no thinking for oneself. Not then.

But Ginny, only seventeen, still listened to her heart and acted, always, in accordance with what it told her. An extraordinary quality in any person at any time, but completely extraordinary in a young woman in the year 1942. At the time, she was simply an enigma to me, and I wasted many hours thinking up ways in which I might set her straight. I did not understand, or recognize, her virtue.

I tried six days in a row to see her, without success, then on the seventh day she came to me.

My mother was at work and the doorbell rang and there was Ginny.

She looked at me and the first words she spoke were, "Do you like vodka?"

Oh, my god, we got rip-roaring, violently drunk. I cannot recall most of that afternoon, but I do remember Ginny laughing so hard she wet her panties and had to put on a pair of my underwear, which sent us off into new hysterics. We sat on the floor of my bedroom spouting the most inane sort of jokes and howling with ridiculous laughter. It was wonderful. Magnificent. For several wild hours we left our troubled, burning planet and lived with grins on our faces that no amount of hard reality could have wiped off. It was a desperate act in a desperate time and to this day I am grateful for it.

We fell asleep sprawled together (and clothed, for sex was not our goal that day) until evening, when my mother called out to let me know she'd come home.

When we woke, Ginny and I lay there together in the twilight, holding hands and beginning to feel rather miserable in our heads and stomachs but at the same time feeling very well, very good indeed. We lay there whispering assorted foolish remarks to one another and smiling and sighing in pleasure. And I knew that she was the best friend I had ever had.

We slipped out of the house while my mother was bathing and took the bus down to the river. Men in uniform were everywhere, looking handsome and brave, and I trembled with the anticipation of being in uniform myself soon. But I didn't tell Ginny. Nor did she tell me how the uniforms made her feel.

We walked and looked at the water, the belching chimneys of the mills, the trains and boats. Pittsburgh was manufacturing artillery at a fever pitch, around the clock. We saw it all, and walked, and made our plans.

Here is what we decided: We would write letters every day, and when I could come home on furlough we would buy an engagement ring together, and when the war was over, we would go to college together. After college we'd marry and move to New York City, where we both believed a richer life waited, and we would live in Greenwich Village and have interesting, flamboyant friends. Then when we tired of the city life, we'd buy a country house somewhere, maybe Vermont, and raise children and rabbits and make a garden and grow old.

We never discussed the possibility that I

might return from the war maimed, or that the war might injure us both in ways we could not foresee, or that the war might even be lost. In our six days apart, Ginny had decided she loved me enough to forgive our different choices and I had decided I loved her enough to follow in any direction she turned.

She had only one request, and that was that she not be required to see me off. She was superstitious about it. She wanted our parting to be in a time and place separate from any trappings of war. She wanted it to be private and personal and to come at the end of a really fabulous time together.

And so it turned out that we said good-bye to each other that very evening. I was willing to follow whatever Ginny's heart dictated, and her heart told her that this night was our strong time and that in strength we should separate.

I took her home and we kissed forever and then I went to war.

M y first painful losses in the war actually occurred when I was no more than twenty-four hours a soldier. I had not expected so sudden a change.

I arrived for basic training in hot Georgia that summer of 1942. Within my first hour there, a sergeant wrapped his hand around my neck and nearly strangled me to death for some stumbling answer I'd made to a question he'd posed. I think in that moment, exactly then, I realized I was completely alone, without help, and that alone I would have to somehow survive. The feeling of desolation was terrible, and I yearned for home and my place in it, though I was beginning to understand I might never have that place again.

From Georgia I was sent to Fort Bragg, North Carolina, for eleven months of artillery training. And then I was shipped to the front.

The Allied plan was to invade Sicily by way of North Africa, and as I rode the troop train through Morocco and Algeria on my way to the fighting, people from the small villages stood by the tracks to wave to all of us. The old men saluted. The young girls blew kisses. We threw our candy to the children. And I loved every minute of it. I loved being a soldier. I loved my country. I loved North Africa. I loved the war and being part of such a wonderful show.

Then, just within the Tunisian border, the joyous townspeople disappeared, replaced by the blackened rubble that artillery had left behind. It stunned us, shocked us into solemnity, threw us back into a serious dread of what lay ahead; and as we boarded the ships that would transport us to an amphibious landing on Sicily's coast, we fell silent.

I am nearly in it, I thought, and I wondered if perhaps we were all just dreaming the same dream.

Our transport hit the beaches and we made our way on foot toward the gunfire. We walked past shelled buildings—homes—that lay in ruins yet were still surrounded by small, lovely fruit trees. I saw birds in those trees.

Ahead of us we could see artillery shells hitting their targets and the great rising of fire, but still we were not completely in yet. The war was just a mile or so away, and I wondered at my simply walking to it, as I might walk to the market or to school. *Today I will walk to the war.*

I remember that we were all clean shaven, our uniforms unsoiled: a handsome group of tidy boys trying to look like soldiers. Nearer the fighting we began to pass men on their way back to the rear, soldiers who had been on the front line, whom we were relieving. They were bloody and dirty and haunted and they watched us go by in our clean uniforms with a mixture of pain and contempt in their faces—and a third thing. A residue of terror, I think.

We passed by artillery emplacements that deafened us with the explosions of shells meant to help clear our way. Then through a small grove of trees. Farther on we could see the village we were to take. And I saw two things that made me think I was surely in a dream.

A castle. Far off, in the hills in the distance.

It was as if I were looking at a postcard from my childhood, the feeling was so familiar, and I thought for a moment that the castle had been built by me. I lined up all the little knights that lay in the box in the basement: CASTLE.

And sheep. Sheep grazing in a nearby meadow as if they were not part of this dream, had chosen not to be included but to wait instead in the sun for the farmer who would soon take them home. I saw sheep standing in a green meadow on this beautiful sunny day.

Then mortar shells began to land in that meadow, and the sheep were hit and lay bloody, half-alive, their bowels spilling among the meadow flowers, and we were all in it. We were all in the Second World War.

I knew a boy, a rifleman, who had wanted so badly to go to the war that he had lain in bed for four days after his eighteenth birthday so he might temporarily gain the extra half inch in height the service required of its new recruits. He got in. Then I expect that, like me, he spent the rest of his time in the army crouching. I hope the half inch in height he lacked wound up saving his life somewhere, as the bullets whizzed above his head.

We were conditioned to think of our enemies in these ways: the Japanese were vicious subhuman jungle creatures who lived on grubs and could see in the dark; the Germans were icy cold, without feeling, mechanical, sick; the Italians were cowards, effeminate, completely ridiculous dandies.

If we could see our enemies in these simple terms, the easier then to kill them. Especially if, as we were repeatedly told, we were doing God's work.

When I had been training those eleven months in North Carolina, safely out of the war, I believed it all. Our divine mission, the promise of a world that would live in harmony, the notion that we would all be finer human beings for our part in this.

I had continued to receive letters from Ginny regularly, but the more I believed in what I was doing, the more distant I felt from her. I remembered her labeling truth as propaganda and resented her lack of patriotism and higher ideals. I wanted her letters to tell me I was doing something important, something heroic. They didn't. And my resentment became so strong that I actually began to dread seeing one of her envelopes. I communicated with her less and less, went to town and kissed beautiful girls, and finally stopped writing to Ginny altogether.

Then I was shipped to North Africa. I didn't take her letters with me.

I stayed in the infantry. Always bound for combat. Always, eventually, out in front. My father would not have believed it. I had been such a slow boy. He forever gently chided me for "bringing up the rear." And there I was, sometimes point man for an entire army.

Only the young are easily shipped to the front. Innocent and hopeful, they willingly go. What they didn't know in the Second World War—what I didn't know—was that once they were sent to the front, for most, there were only three ways to get out again: a severe wound, capture, or death. Those were our only chances of relief, if one may call them that, save the war coming to an end. We didn't know that, once in, the front would close its doors behind us. If we had known, I suspect we might have lost our minds.

After three months of combat, my sureness of why I was there and why we were fighting completely disappeared. I had seen too many dead enemy boys, the color drained from their faces, which, even in death, too closely resembled my own; and as time went on I could not kill them for words. Not for *democracy*, nor *freedom*, and certainly not for *religion*. No one I knew fought for these words.

I killed to keep from dying. I killed to protect the boys in my squad. The history books would eventually say that I killed for the ideals of human liberty. But the history books would be dead wrong.

I wasn't anyone then. I had so little sense of self I don't know that I could have told anyone what I cared about, what I loved, what I wanted. I was quiet, quieter than I'd ever been in my life. I had good friends in the infantry who knew me as one who would watch their backs, drag them to safety, share a foxhole, bandage a wound. Guard their lives as I guarded my own. No one cared whether I was wealthy or well educated, whether my father was a ditch digger or a senator. They loved me, we loved each other, because we all wanted life for ourselves and nothing more.

And there was an intimacy among us, there on the front line, that no soldier working behind the lines would ever know or understand. At times we would be under constant fire and without sleep for days. When finally the attack was over, we collapsed into a pile and slept in each other's arms. In my exhaustion, I did not dream.

On long nights while I waited for the next conflict, I tried to remember my old house, the kitchen, the front porch, my room, and I could rely only on faith that all those things had been real and still existed. I didn't know if I would ever be anything else but an infantryman and in my mind could not fit my uniform, my boots, my gun through the door of that old house. Didn't know where I, muddied and shaken, might sit.

The day the sheep were bloodied in the meadow was the last day I knew the boy in that home.

I am not sure how I survived combat for a week, two weeks, a month, two months. Some days, staying sane was more important to me than staying alive. I saw men of great courage crack under the pressures of warfare. One man, a lieutenant, one day simply told us good-bye and took off walking down the road toward the enemy. He was whistling. He had not gone but half a mile before he was shot dead.

I suffered terrible anxiety attacks during any lull in fighting and was afraid that at any moment I might lose control and start screaming or crap in my pants or shoot everyone in sight. I am certain the others felt such things, too, but the fears were so terrible we could reveal nothing.

And sometimes we did kill each other. In fact, we were often responsible for our own casualties. Sometimes the accidents were large scale, as when our bombers sank enemy transport ships whose hulls were filled with thousands of American prisoners of war. The ships were not marked. Sometimes our bombers attacked German trains carrying hundreds of American boys. Again, unaware of whom they were destroying.

But it was the smaller accidents that became most significant, most damaging to each soldier.

Once, when we were under fire, my best friend suddenly froze with fear as bullets and shrapnel flew all around us. Seeing him there, unprotected, I shoved him into a foxhole and ran on. A mortar shell landed in that hole.

There are the horrifying specters we carry with us forever. A buddy crouching out in the open during a barrage of artillery. "What the hell is he doing?" I yelled, and I ran to him. When I touched him, his head fell off.

The pictures in *Life* may have shown suffering and death to the people back home, but they never showed dismemberment. The shoes with feet and legs up to the knees still standing, and nothing more. The rest of the boy is gone. Or the chest cavity blown wide open so that the heart can be seen, still beating, and the boy to whom the heart belongs reaches out and asks to be helped to die.

The magazine could not bring home the odor of death, of burned flesh and body eliminations and blood. And it would not tell the families back home that the replacements sent to the front line were often so quickly wounded or killed that no one in the platoon even learned their names. The families were never told of the agonizing loneliness of their sons when they died.

Back home, people were making more money than they ever dreamed possible, and they were saving it up to buy houses and cars and refrigerators when the war was finally done. Those who had no sons in combat were dancing at the USO or sitting beside their radios engrossed in tales of cities taken and bombs hitting their marks and enemy ships going down. At the drugstore the young women behind the counters lined up the lipsticks to form a V.

And in Europe someone was sobbing for his mother and searching for his arms.

My letters home were brief. I found that I grew less and less able to be cheerful and reassuring in them, so those that I did write were mainly for the purpose of telling my family I was still alive. The mails, as one might expect, were slow and confused, and months would pass before I'd get a letter from home, though my mother wrote faithfully every week. I also got mail from a few of the girls I'd met in North Carolina, which were cheering in their chirpy, good-humored way. Ginny never wrote. I couldn't blame her, though I did so miss her spirit and her candor. The longer I stayed in the war, the less patience I had for artifice, the better I appreciated her authenticity. I missed her very much.

As the war dragged on through 1944, it became ever more difficult for us all to justify to ourselves why we fought. Though we were supposed to be fighting to preserve freedom and democracy in the world, we had joined up with Russia, and under Stalin, Russia itself was far from being a free and democratic nation. The whole thing became very complex.

As the Germans were weakened later in '44 and pushed farther back toward their homeland, more and more young German soldiers surrendered into our hands. These tired, defeated boys handed us their weapons and we had them remove their boots. There was a strange, almost brotherly feeling inspired by these meetings, and often they would shake our hands or embrace us before we sent them down the road, barefoot, eventually to be picked up and transported as POWs. These meetings made it harder still to work up the necessary distance for killing, and probably only our desperation to get it over with kept us going. Even when our artillery shot down enemy planes, we sometimes found ourselves anxiously scanning the sky for parachutes, hoping the young German pilots had made it out.

When the war began, the conflict had been clearly between Our Side and Their Side, and it was easy to see the enemy as alien, as the animal images painted on the war posters back home. But the longer we all fought, the more commonality we found with each other—all of us, American, British, German, Italian—and the less we found in common with the rest of the world, with anyone who was not a soldier. Some of our boys even exchanged addresses with the young Germans they took prisoner, promising to write once the war was done.

Of course, no one exchanged addresses with any of the members of Hitler's SS. They were truly unreachable, had not a shred of humanity. We would not fully know the reality of their death camps until war's end.

The fight in the Pacific, against the Japanese, was another sort of war entirely. The Bataan Death March early in '42, in which thousands of our men who had been taken prisoner by the Japanese were horribly tortured and murdered on their long walk to the POW camp on the Bataan peninsula in the Philippines, set the tone for the savagery of the battles to come. The Japanese would prove to be unrelenting combatants, refusing under almost any circumstances to surrender, and this would make the Japanese our toughest and most frustrating enemy. And it would push both sides into degradations unthinkable in this life. Most American boys had volunteered simply to avenge Pearl Harbor. The war in Europe had to be fought first, then we could clean up the Japanese. It was infuriating when the Japanese refused to be cleaned up, when the vast expanse of the Pacific theater prevented our getting the damned thing over with. There was, I expect, greater rage aflame in the Pacific war, which had the effect of making any killing there easier.

In Europe, Germany—finally defeated by the sheer devastating amount of our weaponry—surrendered May 8, 1945. We received the news quietly. Some cried. I was so numbed that I could only sit and stare out at nothing, waiting for my orders. We all knew it still wasn't finished. We all knew the Pacific was next. And we knew those of us who had lasted this long had already used up all of our luck.

Spent and shaken, I waited in Europe, as part of the army of occupation, for orders that would probably send me into the invasion of Japan. A rumor circulated that those who had survived the European front would not be asked to fight the Pacific war, but few of us really believed it. We had little hope of any good fortune for ourselves.

By now I was sharply cynical. Any sort of higher purpose to an invasion of Japan, save the rescuing of prisoners and the ending of this hellish war, I could not buy. Roosevelt's admonishments to fight for Freedom died with him in the spring of that year, and now Truman was in charge of rallying the boys to the last front. But the boys weren't boys anymore. I wasn't. My friends who had seen combat weren't. We were the ghosts of boys and we had come to believe in nothing but each other.

From France I managed to phone my mother.

"Mom?" I said when she picked up the phone.

She gave a sob, and for a while nothing was said as she struggled to speak and I struggled to swallow back my own tears.

What does one say after transformation? With some strength and rest, I might have been able to carry us. I might have been able to remember what it was we used to say to each other before I went away. To remember what, back home, I would ask about. But I was without language and without center. I was gone.

My mother asked all the motherly questions: *How are you? Are you well? Are you resting? Do you need anything? When are you coming home?* This last question had been asked so many times in her letters over the last two years. I don't believe any of the mothers understood that their boys on the front lines would not be home until the thing was done. I am certain many of them expected to have their sons home to rest at some point in the war. A war break.

I'm fine. I don't know when I'll be home. How's Dad?

He's fine. Still in California. Maybe you can see him if you come home that way?

Maybe. And Diane?

Fine. Emily is two now. Full of mischief. She has, you know, the nursery.

I'd forgotten the nursery. And the tiny baby my mother had delivered when I was fifteen. The room, like the infant after only two months, had remained silent. But now the room had Emily. A gift from a young man who didn't live past twenty. Diane had bought herself a wedding ring and was treated respectfully as a war widow. She had told me all this in a letter that I'd read somewhere in Italy. Sometime. I don't remember when.

My mother had injured her back at the factory and now stayed home, helping Diane with the child, writing to me, waiting for my father, trying to keep everything the same for us all.

But it was not the same, would never be, and though she did not yet understand this, I knew with absolute certainty that I could not move back into that boy's room and pick up the life I'd left there three years before. I had seen human beings literally shredded to pieces by proximity fuses and burned alive, slowly and agonizingly, by white phosphorus. I could not be that boy anymore, and I didn't want to have to make them understand why. I didn't want talk. I didn't want sympathy. I didn't want a girl or even sex. I had stopped wanting sex a long while back. Food was what we dreamed of in the field. Food was what we wanted when we got back home.

Food, whiskey, cigarettes, and a little oblivion. We sharpened our bayonets and tried to ignore the rumors that said a million more of us were going to die.

And then: Hiroshima.

When the war in Europe began in 1939, both sides had planned not to bomb civilians. It is a funny thing about war: like fire, it has its own life and the longer it lives, the more willful it becomes. Everything starts out quite civilized, the rules of war still uppermost in the minds of the military. Then with each successive dead body, the rage sets in deeper and deeper and soon all the fine intentions of fair play are ablaze.

I have always tried not to say too much about my suffering in the war. In Germany, in the winter, I pulled a twelve-year-old girl from a freezing basement. She had hidden during the bombs. Her legs had frozen. We warmed some water, gently lifted her into a tub, and her feet and lower legs just fell off. Remembering her, I try not to say too much.

I have read many accounts by Americans on the home front who said that the Second World War was a good time. That it was fun, inspiring, exciting. That it gave them jobs, unity, money, opportunities. They say the rationing was hard, but not so bad.

Thirty million Russian people died in the Second World War. Not soldiers—families. Thirty million people. Mothers and grandmothers, fathers and children. They burned and bled, littering the landscape. Their beds burned, and their toys. Their wedding pictures and their babies' carriages.

In Dresden, Germany, our own Allied planes firebombed the city for hours, incinerating everything. Entire blocks were reduced to fine ash. It is difficult to guess how many died. When everything is ash, how does one count? Eighty thousand? A hundred thousand? Children burn to death and leave no traces of themselves. No trace of their glasses of milk, their picture books.

And in the city of Hiroshima, Japan, more than one hundred thousand people died instantly when an atomic bomb—what was that? no one knew at the time—was dropped from a B-29 flying lonely in the sky. People looking up wondered what that bomber was doing there all alone. It wouldn't do much damage, one plane. The children finished their breakfasts. The mothers wrapped up their sleeping infants. And then they all died in a three-thousand-degree oven.

I have tried not to say too much.

My father helped make that single bomb. In the radiation lab at UCLA, where he had been working for nearly three years, he was experimenting with uranium. His duties were limited in scope and he was never told the purpose of his work, though he could guess. He did his job and asked no questions. He believed that an atomic bomb was in the making. He assumed it would be strictly a defensive weapon, deterring any country from invading our mainland. He did not believe it would ever, ever be used, and certainly not on civilians.

He never quite got over this.

And I was in Europe on August 7, 1945— twenty-one years old—believing my luck had surely run dry and having no further hope of surviving the coming invasion of Japan, when off goes this lonely plane with a bomb my father in his small way has helped invent and it is dropped on a city full of children and they and all their families and every living thing in Hiroshima is sacrificed to save me.

Me.

And I don't believe that I ever quite got over this, either.

After the war ended, America made Germany its friend, Russia its enemy, and it helped rebuild Japan. We soldiers had been right all along. The enemy is always interchangeable. Only the boys in the field remain the same, no matter the war. Boys will do the fighting because they are young and still possessed of the best faith. Only the young can be persuaded to die for each other. Only the young can be persuaded this is the only way.

I left Europe and, finally, went home.

Toronto is lovely in summer. I often just sit in the square and watch. People seem happy and I watch them and smile. Just an old man. No one knows where I have been. The young boys who wait impatiently for me to slide through the subway turnstile. The young women who sell tobacco in the drugstore and speak to me in louder voices than necessary. They do not know.

I came home. I cannot speak of this, my homecoming. Cannot. I was a ghost.

I lived with my kind parents, my gentle sister, and the baby for seven months. I did not speak about what I had seen. We attempted only the simplest beginnings: buying new clothes, shoes. Finding a used car I might afford. And the food. I had lost twenty-five pounds. My mother cooked constantly.

My room disturbed me. I could not sleep in it without experiencing impossible anxiety. My father moved a rollaway bed into the music room downstairs, and there I could rest. Nightmares still came. But the room was easier.

I thought, some days, I might start screaming and never stop, and, heart racing, I ran to the park, into the woods, ran and ran and ran until I knew I would not scream. And then I walked home.

Pittsburgh had never seemed to me so noisy, so dirty and cheap. I had seen castles.

There were endless celebrations. Parties, parades, fireworks. Everyone waited for me to sing and to dance, and when I couldn't, my sadness so deep, they were disappointed with me, then guilty in their disappointment, and my loneliness grew. There seemed no right way for any of us. My father's health was poor and he, too, carried his own burdens. Still, he returned to the university, and he found many GIs in his classes with whom he felt a sort of kinship, and his face began to lighten. And in the evening when we sat together in the living room, smoking, thinking, I began to feel again a twinge of that safeness he once could bring to me. I even napped.

Those GIs who had not seen combat—and these were *most* GIs—basked in their heroes' welcome and made plans for their futures and talked at length about the sights of Europe. Worldly wise. Grown.

My parents waited for me to spin a few soldier's adventures at the dinner table, but I had no stories for them. I was sad and quiet and they must have been afraid for me. But, good parents that they were, they did not push.

I visited a few old classmates when I returned, and I walked to the marker in the neighborhood square that bore the names of those friends I could not visit. This marker for the dead seemed oddly out of place amid all the victory bashes, all the new wealth the war had given Pittsburgh.

But there was really no one I could talk to. My squad was scattered across the country— probably, like me, groping their way through conversation.

And Ginny was gone.

I tried to find her, after being home a few

months and gathering at least some of my wits, but her family had moved. I assumed Ginny's father had finally made that money for his house. And I suspected they had quietly returned to Smithville. None of their neighbors could tell me anything. Everyone was so transient in those days, thousands moving in and out of the city. No one knew.

What I wanted very much to tell Ginny, if I saw her, was that she had saved me. I wanted to tell her that in my worst moments of battle I had folded myself up and remembered her. I wanted to thank her for the lovemaking that was the only lovemaking I'd known and tell her how that, too, the memory of her sweetness, had sustained me. I wanted to thank her for the afternoon of vodka. Memories of our hilarity had made me smile during the long monotony of watch.

And I wanted to tell her she had been right. I wanted to explain about my friends—the ones I couldn't save, the ones I didn't bring home— and I wanted her forgiveness for my sins. Anyone else would have told me how heroic I'd been, how brave. They would have told me how proud they were. But Ginny would have looked into my broken face and she would simply have forgiven me. She was so clear.

I didn't go to Smithville to find her. I didn't have enough resolve, was still weak and careful, and could not do it. I was home for seven months and then I asked my parents to help me go to France. I wanted to live in France.

In the war, during the liberation of that country—which was so lovely to me, with its pristine landscape, its cathedrals, its medieval towers—we had been making our way to the front, moving quickly into position, mortar shells exploding several hundred feet in the distance. Beside us was a pasture, and as I crouched and waited for the signal to move forward again, I saw an old French peasant come for a cow in that field, watched him walk the animal away from the noise and the guns, cradling the cow's head in his large hands. Leading the animal to safety.

I could not stay in America because America had not suffered. I needed to be with those whose eyes looked like my own, who had covered their faces and lain in the darkness as bombs fell. I needed to be with those who still felt nervous about walking in an open field and could not help glancing nervously at the sky. I needed the company of people whose hands still shook.

I only barely explained any of this to my

parents. Good parents. They found the money for me and I went.

I lived in France for twenty years. I never returned to America, save for visits to my family. I stayed in a small French village awhile and worked as a laborer. I lived in a goat shed and learned the language. The people were kind to me. And then, again with help from my parents, I went to university. I studied literature. The books were very moving, and I began to find what would become my real life.

After France I lived in England and after England, Greece. There was always some small school in some isolated territory looking to hire a teacher willing to work for pennies so long as he might have solitude and silence.

I tried not to hear about Korea. I tried not to hear about Vietnam. Instead I read poetry to my young students to awaken them to their beautiful lives. Doing this, I found I could be happy.

And now I am spending these years in Toronto. Cities no longer frighten me and I have learned to enjoy the squeaking subway and impatient autos. I relish the fine films I am able to see, and the lovely little cafés, and the young people who walk in dark coats and think about life.

I want to let Ginny know that I am all right. I am an old man. I am sure she checked the neighborhood marker for my name in 1945. She knows I am not dead.

But, Ginny, I want you to know that I am really alive.

And I still love you.